BLACKBERRY FARM

RUSTY THE SHEEP-DOG

Jane Pilgrim

This edition first published in the United Kingdom in 2000 by
Brockhampton Press
20 Bloomsbury Street
London WC1B 3QA
a member of the Caxton Publishing Group

Designed and Produced for Brockhampton Press by
Open Door Limited
80 High Street, Colsterworth, Lincolnshire, NG33 5JA

Illustrator: F. Stocks May
Colour separation: GA Graphics Stamford

Title: BLACKBERRY FARM, Rusty the Sheep-dog
ISBN: 1-84186-040-9

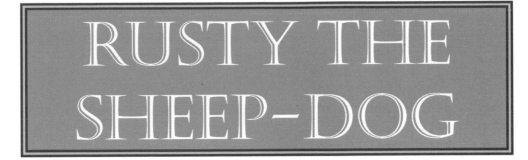

RUSTY THE SHEEP-DOG

Jane Pilgrim

Illustrated by F. Stocks May

BROCKHAMPTON PRESS

Rusty was a brown shaggy sheep-dog, with big brown faithful eyes, a wet black nose, and a very loving heart.

He had been rather a naughty puppy, and sometimes used to chase the chickens and the little ducks. And once he had bitten the tail belonging to Henry the Pig. But Mr Smiles was so cross when he did this that he promised he would never do it again. And he grew into a good trusty dog and worked hard.

Rusty was very fond of Joy and Bob, the two children at Blackberry Farm. They used to have great games together in the farmyard. And sometimes George the Kitten would play with them, too.

Now, Joy had a doll which she
was very fond of, called Amelia.
Mr Smiles had given it to her for
Christmas. And she used to take
Amelia out for walks in her doll's
pram and Rusty would go with
them – down the village or up the
lane to the moor.

But one day Rusty was working
in the fields with Mr Smiles, so Joy
went out by herself. She went
through the village and up the
lane. She thought she would pick
some flowers for her mother.

But two naughty hound puppies,
chasing a cat, rushed out of a gate,
knocked over the pram and ran
away. And when joy looked,
Amelia had gone!

She burst into tears, and ran
back home with her empty pram.
At the gate she met Mr Smiles
and Rusty. "Daddy, Daddy," she
cried, "I have lost my Amelia!"
And with her arms round Rusty's
shaggy neck, she told them what
had happened.

"Rusty will help find her," Mr Smiles said. "Rusty is a good, clever dog." And he patted Rusty's head and showed him the empty pram. "Please, Rusty," Joy cried, "please find my Amelia!" And she hugged him, and he understood.

Rusty went through the village
first, and sniffed all round by the
shop. But there was no Amelia.
Then he went and looked in at
the forge, but there was no
Amelia there.

So he set off up the lane towards
the moor, searching as he went.
On a gate half-way up the lane he
saw Joe Robin. "I'll ask Joe," he
thought. "He knows everything."
So he asked Joe, "Please, do you
know where Amelia is?"

And Joe knew. "Through this field
and over the stile and down to the
hedge at the bottom," he whistled.
"I saw Amelia being carried away
by two naughty puppies."

Rusty went like the wind.
Through the field and over the
stile and down to the hedge at the
bottom. And there was Amelia in a
bed of stinging-nettles!

Rusty carried her tenderly home
to Joy, who hugged him tightly.
Then, clutching the doll, she ran
to tell Mr Smile that faithful Rusty
had found her Amelia.

And Mrs Smiles came out with a big bone for Rusty, because he had been such a clever dog. And Rusty lay in the sun on the doorstep, gnawing his bone and thinking how lucky he was to live at Blackberry Farm.